D0941004

The Bottom of the Boat

Written by Bob Hartman

Illustrated by Michael McGuire

For Mark, a book about the ark. B.H.

To Darlene and the girls and our love of animals. M.M.

VICTOR BOOKS

A Division of Scripture Press Publications Inc.

What was it like in the bottom of the boat?

It was crowded.

"I'm stuck," said the duck.

"It's too tight," shrieked the kite.

"Squeeze in," yelled the pangolin.

"Off my toe!" moaned the hippo.

The dove looked down from her
perch in the rafters.
There were more animals
than she had ever seen.
Why were they there?
What was going to happen?
And why did there have to
be so many of them?

What was it like in the bottom of the boat?

It was noisy.

"Can't hear!" yelled the deer.

"Can't sleep," wailed the sheep.

"Can't think," said the skink.

"What's that sound?" asked the hound.

It was rain.

That's what it was.
From her perch high in the rafters,
the dove had been listening to it
for days—beating, beating, against
the side of the boat. *Would it ever stop?*
she wondered. And what must it
be like, outside? She stuffed
her white head under one
wing to try and shut it out.
Well at least, she thought,
they were safe in here.

What was it like in the
bottom of the boat?
  It was hard to stand up.
  "We're rocking," called the mockingbird.
  "Hang on!" cried the mouflon.
  "We're afloat," announced the stoat.
  "I feel ill," moaned the mandrill.

The boat rocked back and forth. The boat bounced up and down.
The boat heaved forward and backward. And through it all,
the dove clung tight to her perch. For days and days.
For weeks and weeks. For months and months!
And then one day, the boat went bump.
And it stopped.

What was it like in the bottom of the boat?

It was stuffy and boring, and it didn't smell so good.

"Something stinks!" complained the lynx.

"Not me," huffed the kiwi.

"What's that?" sniffed the bobcat.

"Must be you," accused the gnu.

"Can't we go?" asked the rhino.

"Not yet," answered the marmoset.

"Then how long?" cried the binturong.

"I have a plan," announced the man.

And he climbed into the rafters and reached for the dove!
He whispered into her ear.
He told her that she must fly,
fly as far as she could and bring him
any evidence she could find that the earth was dry.
Then he carried her to the very top of the boat,
opened a window, and let her go.

Everywhere! Everywhere she looked there was water.

Nothing but water.

The world was like one enormous sea.

The dove flew for as long as she could

and had almost given up hope of finding anything

but more sea, when she saw it—the tiniest tip

of a branch sticking up out of the water.

She landed on it, tore off a twig,

then carried it back to the boat.

The man waited seven days, then sent her off again.

And this time, she did not return.

What was it like in the bottom of the boat?

It was empty.

"We're there," said the bear.

"We're free!" sang the peccary.

"Let's go!" yelled the bongo.

"Look in the sky," cried the magpie.

And there was the dove, carrying another twig.

But she wasn't headed for the boat this time.

No, she was on her way to a brand new nest.

And behind her, like it was painted on the sky,
    stood a wonder that made the animals
    stop their jumping and running,
    their leaping and digging,
    their crawling and snaking about.
"It's a bow," said the gecko.
"It's an arc," said the lark.
"It's a hat," said the wombat.
"It's. . . a . . . boat!" said the goat.

And sure enough,
that's what it looked like!
A boat.
The bottom of the boat—
turned upside down and
painted party colors—to celebrate
God's fresh-scrubbled, well-washed world.
Yes, that's what it was like. A boat.
The bottom of the boat!

What·Was·It·Like? BIBLE STORIES

The story you have just read is based on Genesis 7–9:17.

KITE PANGOLIN SKINK MOUFLON STOAT

MANDRILL KIWI GNU MARMOSET

BINTURONG PECCARY BONGO GECKO WOMBAT

Art direction: Paul Higdon/Grace K. Chan Mallette
Production: Myrna Hasse
Editing: Liz Morton Duckworth

© 1994 by Victor Books/SP Publications, Inc. All rights reserved. Printed in Mexico

1 2 3 4 5 6 7 8 9 10 Printing/Year 98 97 96 95 94

VICTOR BOOKS A division of SP Publications, Inc. Wheaton, Illinois 60187